OUTCASTS

For the original
'Dealmo' – Clive Deall

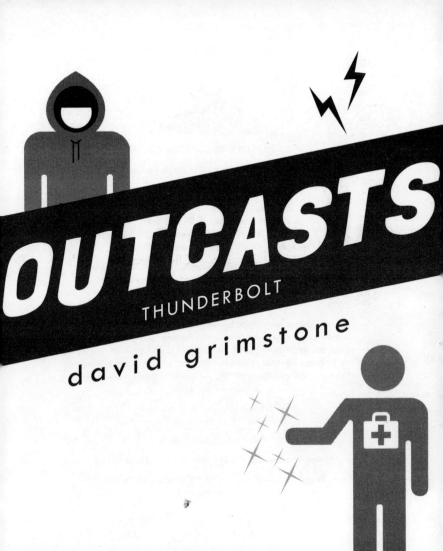

OUTCASTS

THUNDERBOLT

david grimstone

Hodder
Children's
Books

HODDER CHILDREN'S BOOKS

First published in Great Britain in 2017 by Hodder and Stoughton

1 3 5 7 9 10 8 6 4 2

A CIP catalogue record for this book
is available from the British Library.

ISBN 978 1 444 92537 1

Printed and bound in Great Britain by Clays Ltd, St Ives plc

The paper and board used in this book are made from
wood from responsible sources.

Hodder Children's Books
An imprint of
Hachette Children's Group
Part of Hodder and Stoughton
Carmelite House
50 Victoria Embankment
London EC4Y 0DZ

An Hachette UK Company
www.hachette.co.uk

www.hachettechildrens.co.uk

CONTENTS

1

The Sheriff

Butter's Games Shop was always packed on Saturday mornings. This was partly because a shiny new café on the first floor had recently opened, but mostly because the local kids were allowed to bring in their own games and could hang around until their parents started sending out texts about dinner.

The big games room at the back of the shop became a maze of tables, hosting weekly sessions of Magic: The

Gathering, Dungeons & Dragons and even the odd round of Cards Against Humanity (if the sixth formers decided to show up).

On a table in the far corner of the room, Jake Cherish and his friends were on Sheriff of Nottingham, a game where all the players were merchant traders trying desperately to bluff their way past Prince John's resident Bulldog, the Sheriff.

It was Jake's turn to play the villain, and having already lost money against Fatyak and Kellogg, he found himself staring at Lemon's typically blank expression.

'What's in the bag?' he asked her, eyeing the tiny green pouch that concealed her cards.

Lemon broke character and smiled at him. 'Five apples, Sheriff.'

'Five apples?'

'Yes, Sheriff.'

Jake steepled his fingers and stared at her.

'You're lying. Open the bag.'

'Are you sure about that, Sheriff?' Lemon asked, blinking myopically. 'I only ask because you've already lost fifteen gold this round ... and if you're wrong *again*, you're going to end up completely cleared out. In any case, I'm telling the truth. I have five apples: that's it and that's all.'

'Open. The. Bag.'

Fatyak and Kellogg both tensed as Lemon gritted her teeth, pulled open the bag and emptied the cards into Jake's open hands.

'Five apples,' she growled.

Jake counted out the cards, muttered under his breath and shoved his entire gold stack towards her. As he did so, one of the cardboard counters flashed an electric blue before turning into an ant and scurrying towards the edge of the table.

'Nice to see more evidence of your

amazing recovery,' Lemon commented, winking at him. 'But you still owe me one gold.'

Jake's expression hardened and he sat back slightly, staring at his hands as if seeing them for the first time, as if they didn't quite belong to him.

'I don't feel like I've recovered,' he admitted. 'Last summer might seem like just a wild dream to the rest of you, but it feels like a nightmare to me. I've even started to ...'

He trailed off, his eyes now fixed on the door of the games shop.

'You've started to what?' Lemon asked, a sudden tone of concern in her voice.

'Dealmo?' said Fatyak when Jake continued to stare at the door.

It was Kellogg who finally broke the silence, snapping his fingers in front of Jake's eyes and prompting: '*Dealmo*, you in there?'

'What?' Jake looked up. 'Oh, sorry, guys ... I got a bit distracted. Check out the kid at the front counter. That's *him*.'

Fatyak, Kellogg and Lemon abandoned all attempts at subtlety and turned towards the counter, where a younger boy was buying a solo deck of Warcraft cards. He looked extremely shy, staring at his shoes as the girl behind the counter processed his order, and never once glancing at the horde of gamers clearly visible in the room beyond.

'That's who?' Fatyak asked, annoyed that Lemon and Kellogg both looked as if they'd been told something he hadn't.

'Todd Miller's new victim. I think his name is Rufus.' Jake growled. 'I swear that spiteful idiot has no learning curve whatsoever.'

'He's picking on *that* kid?' Fatyak stared at the boy with renewed interest, and gritted his teeth. 'He's in the year below us, right?'

'He is,' Kellogg confirmed. 'And he's *new:* no friends yet. Easy pickings.'

'We really should do something about it, Dealmo,' said Lemon, cracking her knuckles.

Jake nodded. 'Oh, we're going to,' he said. 'We just need to watch him for a while; we need to wait for the right moment.'

2

Judgement Day

Rufus Tern knew he was in trouble the second he left the school grounds: a terror had been creeping up on him since the middle of the dreaded Wednesday afternoon history lesson.

It was no secret that Mr Middleton couldn't control his lessons, but Wednesday afternoons were a nightmare on an entirely different level. On Wednesdays, Middleton stood aside for a series of hopeless supply teachers, giving the class clowns a chance to rule the room.

These idiots were rarely a problem for Rufus ... but Todd Miller was.

Miller didn't pick at people every day, and his only required audience consisted of the two gormless stooges who followed him around everywhere, and whatever hapless victim had attracted his attention. Miller might not speak to this chosen wretch for five or six weeks, but then – one day – he would sit down quietly next to the selected target and it would start.

Miller loved to pick on new kids, and Rufus had only arrived at the school one month into the second year. He'd been told, of course: any kid who suffered the attentions of Miller was always sure to pass on a warning to the next newcomer, as one of the first things that was really 'worth knowing'.

To make matters worse, Rufus had practically been emblazoned with a target on the day he'd arrived in school: having a dad doing five years in a maximum-security prison might have deterred kids from attacking you in old Hollywood movies, but in the real world it made you a total prize.

He'd already suffered a few minor beatings at the hands of a spiteful little mob at the end of double drama, but

Todd Miller had stalked him for weeks, making threat after threat after threat.

Today, Rufus had drawn the short straw ... and he knew it.

Miller sat down next to him, and about twenty minutes into the lesson quietly leaned over and said:

'Today's the day. You're dead after school.'

Then he returned to the table he and his sniggering mates occupied and carried on with his work. He stopped several times to shout across the class, asking Rufus for a pencil or to make some casual comment about a question in the textbook but, when the bell sounded he looked over and smiled in a way that scared Rufus so much that he couldn't even quantify it.

Rufus had snatched up his bag and run, actually *run* out of the history block and across the school grounds to the front entrance. He'd run until he was three streets away and could barely even breathe.

Then he'd found himself faced with a difficult decision: should he go home via Royal Road or the storage yard?

If he went for Royal Road, he risked walking right through the territory Miller always occupied after school. Even though the little fiend couldn't possibly have got in front of him, Rufus was reluctant to chance the more obvious route.

But that left the storage yard.

On a good day, the storage yard was full of people depositing, picking up or checking on their stuff. On a bad day, it was a complete wasteland ... and wastelands offered a prime hunting ground for creatures like Miller. It was a quicker way home, but if he was cornered in that place, there would literally be no escape.

Rufus decided to take the risk, but quickly discovered – to his horror – that the place was utterly deserted.

He can't be here already, Rufus told

himself, the words repeating in his head like a mantra. *He can't be here this fast.*

A sort of grim confidence flickered inside Rufus at the thought, but it was soon dissolved.

He was about halfway down a narrow avenue of mini garages and giant blue shipping containers when Miller suddenly, impossibly, stepped out from behind one at the end of the stack.

'Why can't you just leave me alone?' Rufus shouted loudly, hoping someone, somewhere would hear. 'I haven't done anything to you. I'm just going home!'

Miller sniffed, shrugged and folded his arms.

'Alright,' he said. 'Go on then. Go home.'

Miller bared teeth encased in braces and held the smile until Rufus tried to speak.

'P-please-'

'I thought you said you wanted to go home?' he growled. 'So ... go home.'

Rufus took a step back and turned round, but Miller's two friends had sidled out from behind the storage stacks and were blocking the path.

'Not that way, kid' Miller spat on the ground. 'If you want to go home, this way is quicker. All you have to do is get past *me*.'

Rufus was shaking so badly that he had to ball his hands into fists in order to hold on to his school-bag. He felt his stomach doing somersaults and his mouth drying up as he tried to think of something, anything, that would make Miller go away.

It was no use: there was no alternative to just walking past Miller and taking whatever punishment he'd chosen to dish out.

Rufus took the long walk, putting one foot in front of another in a series of awkward movements that made him feel as if he was made of glass.

All the while, Miller just watched

him, hands thrust deep into his pockets.

Rufus passed so close to the boy that he could hear Miller breathing and felt sure a punch would floor him at any moment ... but it didn't.

He moved through Miller's available tackle zone and was almost clear of it when he heard a low, guttural growl, the sort a dog would make.

His heart began to pound.

Turning round was a mistake, he should have made a run for it.

The shove caught Rufus square in the middle of the chest and he flew backwards. He dropped his bag, twisted round and toppled over it in an attempt to flee, but Miller was upon him, pushing him down for a second time. His friends swooped in, their combined laugh making them sound like a pack of rogue hyenas.

'When you get home,' came the oily voice as Miller circled his prey, 'and your mummy asks you why you're all messed up, you can tell her that you weren't just mullered, you were *Millered*.'

The group burst out laughing and leaned on each other for support.

'P-please don't!' Rufus put up a hand to cover his face.

'Of course, you could go straight home and tell your dad ... if he wasn't in *prison*.'

Miller reached down and snatched hold of Rufus ...

... or he would have done if he'd still been standing there.

A blurry shape hit Todd Miller hard, lifting him off his feet and slamming him into the bulk of the nearest shipping container. The noise of the impact was like a sudden thunderclap. Rufus didn't even get a chance to see what happened to Miller's two mates. One second they were standing there laughing, the next they were scrambling to their feet and running away so fast that clouds of dust formed up behind them.

The world seemed to shimmer for a

second, as if time had come to an abrupt pause.

Then reality came back, with a bang.

Driven hard into the container, Miller blew out so much air that he wretched and almost spewed.

The figure that had cannoned into him withdrew lightning-fast, crouching as if ready to lunge forward again at a second's notice.

'Sorry to interrupt,' said a voice from somewhere on top of the stack. 'I understand you were quite keen for a bit of three-on-one, hand-to-hand combat. That's fine with us, we love a good scrap, but there's not much victory in a trio of seniors ambushing some poor, defenceless kid. If he's such a loser, why not just fight him on your own? I mean you *can* do that, right?'

Miller choked as he tried to catch his breath, but he was still dry heaving on to the ground with every attempt he made to stand up. His tortured gaze travelled to the top of the stack, where a boy he immediately recognised was standing with his hands in his pockets, smiling down on the scene.

'Take your time, Miller. Lemon only gave you what she calls a "love tap" but I guess she doesn't know her own strength.'

The girl straightened from her crouched pose and removed the hood she'd been wearing.

Miller rallied for another lungful of air, found his feet and launched himself at her. Luckily Lemon turned at exactly the right moment, landing Miller on the ground, face first.

'Lemon! Give him a chance to get up. How can he "Miller" anyone from down there?'

The girl sighed. 'Oh, come on, Dealmo. I haven't laid a finger *on* him.'

Miller scrambled to his feet, but slipped in the attempt and hit the ground again, even harder. He let out a yelp that might have been an actual sob, and practically deflated.

'We're not waiting around to take turns attacking,' Jake added. 'If we did that, we'd be no better than you ... and trust me, Todd, we are *so* much better than you.'

Rufus watched with fascinated horror as the boy who had terrified him mere moments ago made a final, desperate bolt for the end of the stack.

He ran into the biggest kid Rufus had ever seen and slid down his belly like a cartoon character. The newcomer, who was wider than he was tall, smiled and cracked his knuckles.

'Oh, sorry. Fatyak doesn't want you to go home that way. Try the other direction. I know your house is by the station but the walk will give you some valuable thinking time.'

Lost, humiliated and bewildered, Miller began to shuffle forward ... and stopped. 'What do you want from me, Cherish?' he mumbled.

Jake stepped off the edge of the stack and floated, actually *floated* to the ground. He grinned when Miller's jaw dropped open at the sight.

'Before you go,' said Jake, striding up to the bully and snatching hold of his shirt just below the neck, 'I'm going to ask you for the very last time to stop picking on the new kids. Oh, and just in case your memory doesn't stretch back all the way to last summer, here's a quick reminder about what happens when you cross the Outcasts.'

Lemon suddenly darted forward and drove her fist into the shipping container so hard that the metal bent. Her knuckles flushed and began to bleed, but she held the injured fist up for Kellogg, who produced a soft circle of blue light that completely healed the wound.

Fatyak turned to face away from the group before somersaulting backwards and flipping several times, landing finally mere centimetres from Miller's feet.

Jake drew the boy's ear close to his mouth.

'I can do all that and more,' he whispered.

He shoved Miller for the first few steps, but the boy soon picked up the pace and found his own way out of the storage yard. He was nothing more than a distant speck on the horizon when Rufus finally turned to the Outcasts and said:

'Th-thank you. Thank you SO much. Y-you guys are incredible!'

Jake smiled at the boy and let out a long, exasperated breath.

'Don't big us up too much,' he said. 'There's a price to these ... *gifts* we have.'

Fatyak stepped forward and put a reassuring hand on the boy's shoulder. 'Don't listen to him. It was worth all the effort to see that look on Miller's face. Now, what's your name, kid?'

'R-Rufus. Rufus Tern.'

'Rufus,' he said. 'We've been watching you for a while ... and you're not like any of the other kids Miller bullies. To be honest, you seem like a bit of a loner—'

'That's cool if it's your choice,' Lemon cut in, stepping in front of the boy. 'But I'd bet you find it pretty difficult to make friends ...'

Rufus fixed her with an angry stare, but his cheeks flushed red.

'How would you like to hang out with us?' Jake asked. 'You can pop by Lemon's after school: that's where we hang out. Fatyak can give you the address. What do you say?'

Rufus looked from one member of the group to another.

'Are you kidding?' he said. 'That would be totally *awesome*!'

3

The New Arrival

Lemon's tree house had been the unofficial meeting place of the Outcasts since before Jake had found the box that had dramatically changed their lives.

Now it was covered from floor to ceiling with newspapers. Even the makeshift couch looked like it was made of papier mâché. Only the sun, shining in through the single circular window, revealed the fact that there was actually some sort of material underneath the printed sheets.

On the floor in the middle of the room were three giant packets of sweets, a large bowl of crisps and a litre bottle of Coke. It appeared that none of them had been touched.

Jake lay in one corner of the room, nodding in and out of sleep and squinting at the sunlight.

He felt exhausted, but not quite as exhausted as Fatyak, who was actively snoring away like a high-speed train at the other end of the room.

Somewhere in between the two, Lemon lay looking up at the articles covering the ceiling. They ranged from reports of minor burglaries to front-page coverage of international events.

'Dead ends,' Lemon muttered, shaking her head and sniffing. 'Sooo many dead ends. Maybe newspapers aren't the way to go.'

Jake turned his head and yawned. 'There's no giving up,' he said. 'You can't expect a secret organisation like the Reach to broadcast the stuff they do. That's why it's important to keep looking for them.'

Lemon forced herself up on to her elbows.

'Fatyak *destroyed* the box,' she said. 'Besides, we have no idea exactly what that *thing* has done to us in the long run ... or if we're ever going to stop feeling like this.'

Jake watched her carefully. 'You're still not well?'

'Not well? Ha!' Lemon rolled on to her stomach. 'I can punch down a wall and tip cars over, then a day comes along when I can barely stand up.'

'None of us are right,' said Kellogg, appearing at the trapdoor in the floor of the tree house and climbing inside. 'Dealmo has headaches he tries to hide, Fatyak needs *three* alarm clocks to wake him up in the morning, Lemon has a cold that never goes away and I have cuts and bruises that take weeks to heal.

That is why we have to track down the Reach and get some more answers about Pandora's box and about why we still have superpowers.'

Fatyak sat up and rubbed his eyes.

'What's that?' Jake asked, as he and Lemon both took note of the little key-ring Kellogg was holding. 'It's not another panic button, is it?'

Kellogg had provided each member of the group with tiny wireless buttons that vibrated and emitted a tracking frequency whenever any one of them was pressed. Fatyak hadn't managed to get a full night's sleep since Kellogg had issued them.

'It's an improved version: this one has a tiny screen with an arrow that flashes in the direction you need to go to find the alert. It's like a mini satnav, but way more accurate. I made one for each of us, because—'

'No.'

Jake and Lemon both glared at Fatyak, but Kellogg simply rolled his eyes and sighed.

'Oh come on, dude, we *have* to use these things. I worked for ages on them!'

Fatyak shook his head.

'Not a chance. I keep pressing mine by mistake in the middle of the night. The noise is mental, and then I have to spend ten minutes calling everyone's mobiles to let them know I'm OK.'

Lemon snorted. 'Most people don't sleep with their house keys!'

'Fatyak does,' said Jake, nodding at his friend. 'He thinks that weird little voodoo doll on his key-ring protects him while he's asleep.'

'Shut up, Dealmo! It does!'

'Well, I'm taking one,' said Lemon. 'It's good to keep us all connected.'

Jake nodded.

'Couldn't agree more. I'll take one. Thanks, Kellogg.' He glanced sideways at Fatyak.

'What? I don't want the stupid thing.'

43

'Listen, it was *you* who destroyed the box. If Nathan Heed ever gets out of prison—'

'Hello?'

The Outcasts all turned to look at the trapdoor, where the nervous face of Rufus Tern was staring up at them.

'Y-you said I could come over if I was passing? I rang at the door. Lemon's mum said you were out here. Is it OK to come up?'

'Welcome to the Outcasts' clubhouse, Rufus.' Jake held out a hand and pulled the younger boy inside. 'You're a bit late, as we're just packing up. Our year had a free study day.

Want something to eat? We've got loads ... but, to be fair, that's because Fatyak fell asleep.'

'Hey!'

Rufus smiled, but his eyes went straight to the laptop.

'I couldn't help overhearing about the prison stuff,' he said with a reluctant smile. 'A-are you guys in some sort of trouble? You know, because of the stuff you do?'

Jake grabbed a plastic cup and poured out some Coke for their new arrival, while Fatyak reluctantly offered the boy some of his sweet stash.

'You know anything about

Pandora's box, Rufus?'

The boy looked up, his eyes practically glowing.

'I love Greek mythology,' he replied. 'Pandora's box was a trick disguised as a wedding present. Zeus gave it to Pandora because he wanted to get back at her husband, Epimetheus ... and that was only because his brother stole the first fire from the gods! Actually, it wasn't a box at all: it was a large jar. My mum says—'

'Trust me,' Jake interrupted. 'It was a box.'

'OK,' said Rufus carefully. 'I'm just saying that my mum—'

'We know it was a box because we found it,' interrupted Kellogg, 'and we opened it.'

Rufus waited a second, but nobody else made any attempt to speak.

'I don't get the joke,' he said quietly. 'This *is* a joke, right?'

Jake shook his head, setting off a round of very serious murmurs.

'B-but Pandora's box is supposed to contain all the evils of the world. I mean, I know it's pretty grim out there with all the wars and terrorism and stuff, but surely if you'd opened the actual Pandora's box we'd all be dragged off to hell by a bunch of demons or something?'

'The box,' said Lemon, picking up a piece of metal she'd bent almost in half, 'gave us the power to do the things we do.'

Rufus blew out a heavy, exasperated breath and scratched his head.

'But Pandora's box is a poisoned chalice! My mum said there's this version of the story in the National Archaelogical Museum of Athens where everything that comes out of the box looks really good but ultimately turns to death and darkness in the end. That was, er – why are you all looking at me like that?'

Fatyak, Kellogg and Lemon were

all glaring at the boy, but Jake stepped forward, thrust both hands into his pockets and took a deep, measured breath.

'They're looking at you like that because the box was a poisoned chalice.'

'Was?' Rufus smiled nervously. 'What happened to it?'

'Fatyak hurled the cursed thing off a roof, but the effects didn't really disappear ... they just dwindled a bit. Now we're all ill in different ways, as if the box is starting to take something back. I know you can't tell by looking at us, but – seriously – we're in bad shape. We need to find the people who owned the box before us.'

Fatyak interrupted. 'A really shady group called the Reach, who have already sent a bunch of agents to kill us once.'

'Who are they?'

Fatyak shrugged. 'We honestly don't know whether they're fanatical guardians of ancient artefacts or just a well-organised network of treasure hunters. Either way, they're bad news. Sadly, we have no leads whatsoever to where they might be.'

Rufus swallowed a few times, then slowly lowered himself on to the floor of the tree house and accepted the plastic cup from Jake. He took three generous gulps before wiping his mouth with the back of his hand.

'How come you weren't all captured? D-did you guys kill the agents?'

Jake shook his head.

'We're not murderers,' he whispered. 'Although the leader of the bunch would gladly have put us all in the ground.'

'We're trying to find out more about the Reach, but it's hard going,' Kellogg admitted. 'To be honest, we can't even work out how a group like that came to acquire something as ancient as Pandora's box.'

Rufus whistled between his teeth.

'Look, I might not be able to help you fight a load of assassins,' he said, 'but if the Reach are involved in collecting stuff that belonged to the Ancient Greeks, then it might just be fate that you saved me from Todd Miller. My mum's an expert on ancient artefacts; she's always talking about them for her job. My mum signed me up for extra history, which means I get to go on trips with all five study groups whenever they do field work. I swear to you, I'll piece together every shred of evidence I can find about the box. I might be able to help you guys.'

The Outcasts glanced at each other.

'Well, we certainly haven't found anything in Kellogg's catalogue of files,' Fatyak pointed out with a grin. 'He practically downloaded the entire INTERNET for us to search through. You know, I reckon if Rufus here thinks he can be an asset to the most awesome group of superheroes since the Fantastic Four, we should give him a chance to prove it.' He turned to the boy and gave him a friendly pat on the shoulder. 'Hell, I bet we can even get Kellogg to give you the group panic button.'

'Sure thing!' Kellogg practically raced across the tree house to deposit the little gadget in Rufus's unresisting hand. 'This is something we use to contact each other in case of dire emergency.'

'Or when Fatyak rolls over in bed,' Lemon added with a grin. 'Hey, Rufus. If you come and see us at the same time tomorrow, we should be able to hang around a bit longer.'

'Sure, OK! Thanks again, guys. It's pretty cool to have people to hang out with.'

'Any time.'

Rufus said his goodbyes to the group, hurrying after Fatyak down the tree-house ladder. 'You going straight home?' he asked tentatively. 'Only I wondered if we could swap mobile numbers.'

Fatyak jumped down from the bottom rung of the ladder and clapped some dust from his hands.

'Kellogg's panic button not enough of a connection for you?' he asked, grabbing a handset from his jacket while giving a lopsided grin. 'Here's mine. Lemon's is just below it, followed by Dealmo's and Kellogg's. Hope you're not a text spammer, Rufus.'

'I've only sent three texts from my new phone,' the boy confided, 'and they were all to my mum.' He grabbed his own handset and copied out the numbers. 'Are you going straight home now?'

Fatyak nodded.

'Yeah, although I might get a burger on the way home.'

'Cool. Want to see where I live first?'

'Er ... yeah, OK. Why not.'

Rufus hated going home. It always seemed like hours until his mum returned from work, and the house was still full of moving-in boxes. He'd asked many times if he could help unpack stuff so they'd have at least *one* room that wasn't cluttered with boxes, but his mum was really particular about what went where.

'She's always been a control freak,' he told Fatyak when the boy remarked on the boxes stacked outside Rufus's room. 'But it's been a lot worse since Dad went to prison. Now she has to have everything just where she wants it. She wants us to unpack everything together, eventually.'

'Right.' Fatyak looked at a large photograph of the family that occupied pride of place on the little table beside the bed. 'What happened with your dad? What did he do?'

Rufus stared at Fatyak for a while.

'It doesn't matter,' the older boy said, clapping a hand on his new friend's shoulder, 'and it would never stop us being friends. I'm just ... interested, that's all. You guys look so happy in that picture.'

Rufus looked away.

'We were,' he said quietly. 'But my dad ... well ... I guess he beat up some guys.'

'Did they deserve it?'

'Kinda. They were robbing this lady outside a shop, and he, well, you know, he stopped them.'

Fatyak frowned. 'He went to prison for *that*?'

'Yeah. The thing about my dad is that he's got a bit of a temper. He doesn't really know when to stop. It took three policemen to get him away from the muggers. Plus, he did quite a lot of stupid stuff when he was younger ... so I guess the courts just decided he was a bad guy.'

Fatyak sniffed and nodded. 'That sucks, dude.' He glanced around the room. 'So it's just you and your mum?'

'Yeah,' said Rufus quietly. 'She works a lot though. She's a curator and a duty manager at the museum.'

'The big one? In town?'

'Yeah.'

'Cool. Er ... listen, I should be heading home. I kinda need to catch up on some sleep.'

'Do you have to go right now?' Rufus tried to keep the desperate edge out of his voice. 'It's just that Mum isn't back for another few hours, so if you wanted to hang out for a bit, that'd be cool. You don't have to though.'

Fatyak glanced at the clock and smiled.

'Do you have an Xbox One?'

'No, but I've got a PS3.'

'Two controllers?'

'Yeah!'

'Let's do it.'

4
Exhibit F8

The tour guide at the Mendlesham Museum of Ancient History was desperately trying to move the school group along to the next exhibition, but one particularly annoying child would just not stop asking questions. They came thick and fast, and covered such a wide variety of topics that they were almost impossible to field. When the girl's hand went up for the tenth time in as many minutes, he sighed despondently, counted to five under his breath and nodded.

'Yes?'

The girl tucked a lock of hair behind her ear and pointed at a cracked and broken urn.

'How does the donkey on the side of Exhibit C1 connect with Zeus again?'

'Um ... thank you, Scarlett. Basically, it—'

'Charlotte.'

'I'm sorry?'

'My name, sir. It's Charlotte, not Scarlett.'

'Oh, OK, *Charlotte*. Well, the urn at C1 isn't actually depicting an aspect of Zeus. You're getting it confused with the vase at E3. The *donkey, Silenus,* is associated with another legend entirely, that of King Midas.'

A flurry of hands shot up, and the tour guide found himself answering questions on the king and his talent for turning everything he touched into gold.

After what seemed like an age, the class's great thirst for knowledge had been quenched and every hand in the room went down ... every hand except one.

The tour guide folded his arms impatiently but to his sudden relief he saw that the raised arm belonged to a child he knew quite well.

'Oh, hello, Rufus. What's your question?'

The boy smiled and glanced down at his pad.

'Sir, how is the urn connected with the gold tube at F8? I see they're both listed under The King Midas Legend, but there's no plaque under that one.'

'Well, in fact ...'

The tour guide stared at the golden cylinder that sat on a podium at the far end of the display. He blinked a few times and rubbed his eyes before leaving his stool in order to closely examine the display.

'I'm not sure about this one, Rufus,'

he admitted. 'It must have arrived over the weekend. We sometimes keep things in storage for various archaeological groups, but it must have been put on display by mistake. That case is supposed to contain a diorama on Pandora's box.'

At the front of the group, Rufus Tern suddenly looked up from his notepad.

'But, sir ...' the girl interrupted.

'That's enough questions for today,' said the class teacher, stepping forward. 'I'll make sure the correct notes on it are included in your information packs first thing on Monday morning. Now, we really must move on!'

As the group began to shuffle out,

Rufus hung back.

The guide put on a pair of spectacles and squinted at the tube in the case. Then he motioned to a stern-looking woman behind the front desk who Rufus recognised as his mother's assistant.

'I don't know what it is,' she muttered, joining him by the case. 'It was delivered by the Regional Director of Operations on Friday. We were told to house it as an open exhibit in order to divert the wrong sort of attention from it, whatever that means. It's a real oddity though. Even Mrs Tern isn't sure of its origin.'

The guide frowned.

'If we're supposed to divert

attention from the thing, wouldn't it have been a better idea to house it in the artefact vault?'

'Apparently not,' the woman advised, taking a letter from the printer and sliding it across the desk towards her colleague. 'Didn't you get the memo? The vault was raided at the weekend.'

'What? I thought the vault was supposed to be impenetrable.'

'Yes. Evidently so did the management. It just goes to show you that incredible things can happen on any given day if you have the right equipment, and these folks definitely did.'

'What did they take?'

'That's the strange part. They didn't take anything.' She tapped on the glass. 'I think they might have been looking for this.'

Rufus watched the pair as their conversation reduced to hushed whispers. Eventually he joined the rest of his study group, but he spent the rest of the afternoon exchanging texts with the Outcasts. It was quickly decided that the group would visit the museum in the morning, in order to get a closer look at the cylinder. Rufus couldn't help but feel a tiny flicker of pride. After all, he'd made his first potentially useful contribution to the group.

5
The Late Shift

At midnight, the museum's newly appointed nightwatchman carefully walked the corridors using the exact route he had been given by his predecessor.

After repeating the circuit twice, he diverted and moved into a storeroom behind the manager's office, where he proceeded to methodically disable the special alarm system on the inner sanctum of the museum's private archive. Then he spent the best part of an hour dismantling every artefact on the restoration list and a further fifty minutes opening sealed lockboxes with the aid of a small machine.

Eventually, finding no satisfaction on his exhaustive hunt, he snatched up the communicator at his belt, pressed a button on the top and rasped:

'Look, I don't care what the stupid computer says. I'm telling you it's not here. I've looked in every possible hiding place.'

The scratchy voice that replied sounded like it was coming from many miles away, but in fact came from the company's unmarked van parked opposite the museum entrance.

'Have you tried inside—'

'IT'S THERE!' Colonel Bleach's voice suddenly cut across the line of communication. 'I'm looking at a fat blue dot on my screen: that's a clear indicator.'

'Sorry, sir! I didn't think you were—'

'Just follow my instructions, Alvarez. I don't pay you to think.'

'Yes, sir!'

'Right.' The Colonel's harsh voice seemed to hesitate for a second. 'Firstly, stay still so that we can run a scan of the building and lock on your place inside it.'

'If you can do that, sir—'

'We didn't do it earlier because the

museum security can detect the intrusion, initiating a secondary protocol which could alert the management. As soon as we do that, the entire operation might fail. So, listen *carefully*.'

'Yes, sir!'

'We will have your location in seconds.'

⚡

The telephone in the hallway was an old-fashioned one with a ridiculously loud ring.

It never rang like this though – in the middle of the night.

The woman emerged from the bedroom and half stepped, half fell down the flight of stairs, her eyes bleary and her hands working frantically to keep her matted hair out of her face.

She reached down and snatched up the receiver, checking the landing to make sure that the noise hadn't woken the house's only other occupant. Fortunately, there was no sign of him.

'Who is this?' she said wearily. 'Do you have any idea what time it is?'

'Sarah, it's Malcolm.'

The woman put one hand on the small table that supported the telephone and tried to clear her throat. Her boss didn't call her very often, and he wasn't the sort of man who bothered people unnecessarily.

'Wh-what's wrong?'

'We just got an automated call from the online security program at the museum. I wouldn't usually ask this, but could you get in with your software and cancel the secondary protocol? Sorry, but I'm up in Scotland and you're the only other member of staff with an all-access pass.'

'Don't you want me to go to the museum to check it? I know the system has been shaky lately, but—'

'You and I both know that this is

going to be some pointless test from regional to show how well we're trained in security, but we have the new guy on night watch who I trust absolutely. If you end up down there, you might as well go straight into your day shift. Just override the protocols on your laptop. You can do that, right?'

Sarah looked to the top of the stairs, where her son had appeared in his Star Wars pyjamas, a confused look on his face.

'Um ... of course! I'll get on it immediately.'

'Brilliant. Thank you so much.'

She replaced the receiver, and

cast a quick glance towards her son on the landing.

'Mum?' he said. 'What's happened? What's going on?'

Sarah hurried up the stairs towards him.

'Go back to bed, Rufus. It's just a false-alarm trigger from the museum. I'm going to log on quickly and shut it down.'

Rufus nodded blearily and went back to bed. But as soon as he'd closed the door behind him, he snatched up his phone and called Dealmo.

No answer.

He tried Lemon but her phone was off.

Kellogg's just rang and rang.

Finally he called Fatyak and got through to voicemail. 'It's Rufus!' he whispered. 'I think the Reach are hitting the museum tonight. Right now, in fact. My mum just got an emergency call from her work. I don't want to cause you guys any panic, but ...'

He trailed off, suddenly remembering the gadget Kellogg had given him.

'No worries,' he finished. 'I know what to do.'

Then he hung up and did something he later realised might have been the most stupid thing he'd ever done: he

77

packed a bag and sneaked out of the house.

⚡

'Left at the next junction.'

Alvarez stopped dead and frowned.

'That would take me into the main museum,' he protested. 'I doubt they'd put something this important in an actual display.'

'LEFT. AT. THE. NEXT. JUNCTION.'

'Sir,' he said gloomily, turning and ploughing through the set of heavy double doors that led to the front-of-house displays. He hadn't liked Colonel Bleach from the moment they'd met, and the situation wasn't improving.

'Now, head down the stairs, take the first left and the second right. The piece should be directly in front of you.'

There was a sizeable delay before Alvarez's voice rang out across the communicator.

'Holy mother of ... It's here! They've actually got it on display behind a single sheet of glass!'

'That's because they don't have any idea what's inside it! Now, you need to cut out the middle of the glass. Do not, on any account, smash the barrier.'

'But, sir ...'

'Just use the laser.'

'I left the laser in the van. We thought it would be in a lockbox, so I only took in the miniature explosives.'

A few seconds passed in grim silence. Then, using a decidedly measured tone, Colonel Bleach said:

'Open the storeroom door. I'll send Slud in with the laser.'

'You can't, sir. You had me fix all those security beams over the crates, remember?'

'I'll turn them off. Now, stop arguing, damn it. I'm not used to having every second order I give questioned. If I tell you to do something, you DO it.'

6

Intruder Alert

The mountain bike screeched to such an abrupt halt in the museum car park that Rufus nearly went straight over the handlebars. This was partly because he'd been going so fast, but mostly because one of his hands had been entirely occupied by keeping the panic button firmly pressed the whole way to the museum.

He locked up his bike, hurried across the deserted ground, and walked up to

the delivery entrance of the building —
a large garage door that he'd seen his
mum operate with an electronic key on
her first delivery shift.

It was half raised.

Rufus felt a sudden rush of
adrenalin as he realised that every scene
his fevered imagination had conjured on
the ride from home could be about to
play out in front of him.

There might be an actual raid
taking place on the museum, by real-
life bad guys, who might very possibly
belong to a genuine organisation of dark
intent.

It was like the movies, only real.

What the hell am I doing here?

His mind raced, finally settling on how frightened and worried his mother would be when she woke up to find him gone.

Except that the Outcasts would come to sort everything out, just like they had done in the storage yard, and he'd be home by morning. They had to be on their way...

Rufus looked down at the little gadget in his hand and felt the first flicker of a doubt.

What if Kellogg's panic button didn't actually work? What if nobody was coming? What if he was on his own? He couldn't call the police. As soon as any of the authorities were involved, the Outcasts would never get their answers.

Returning his attention to the half-open door, Rufus found himself mesmerised by the sight. It was as if the danger and the *idea* of being a hero was drawing him towards the museum. He literally could not turn away.

Rufus took a deep breath and swallowed. Then he counted to ten, ducked beneath the door and disappeared into the darkness beyond.

A single low-level, wall-mounted light bathed most of the room in shadow, but Rufus could see that a path had been cleared between the larger crates, which had all been shoved against the wall. This wasn't out of the ordinary as far as he could tell. He'd visited the museum once during a delivery and the space was often kept clear for incoming exhibits.

Rufus suddenly found himself doubting the situation. What if one of the museum staff had decided to put in some extra after-hours work on a display?

He covered his mouth with a shaking hand.

How stupid will I feel if I have to tell all the Outcasts and my mum that I made a mistake and I've done this all for nothing?

Rufus stopped dead.

The two biggest crates stacked against the door leading to the museum beyond had a network of glimmering red lines suspended between them, creating a cobweb of eerie light that looked like the work of millions of tiny, radioactive spiders.

Rufus blinked, tightly shutting his eyes and opening them again, trying to dispel the strange image as an optical illusion ... but a second glance revealed that the effect was being produced by four boxes sitting on top of the crates in pairs, throwing out beams of light.

This was definitely not part of the museum's security system. It looked temporary, far too improvised to be anything other than a portable solution. Moreover, the beams literally covered the small area between the crates and the doorway beyond, rising to a height of maybe six feet.

Rufus saw that there was no way under the network of light but that a sizeable gap would allow someone to drop from the metal walkway above to *behind* the left crate, affording an entrance to the door. The only problem was that there was no way on to the balcony that didn't involve climbing up a sheer brick wall. Rufus had never been particularly agile.

Approaching the right-hand box from an angle, Rufus squinted at the little pair of contraptions. Each one appeared to have two buttons on the top: one red, one yellow.

Red always signifies danger, Rufus told himself. *The yellow might be some sort of interrupt switch.*

Rufus carefully reached out a finger and was less than a centimetre away from pressing the button when a cold, sharp voice said:

'I wouldn't do that if I were you.'

Swallowing, sweating and trying to stop himself from shaking, Rufus slowly turned himself around to face the voice.

'What the hell do you think you're doing, Rufus?' said Fatyak, stepping under the door in a thick duffle coat that completely failed to hide his pyjamas. 'Have you got some sort of death wish, or are you just really, really stupid?'

'Fatyak! Boy, am I glad to see you! Listen, I can explain.'

'You don't need to explain,' the older boy snapped. 'You think the Reach are here in the museum. See? I listened to your message, but did you listen to *us?* Have you forgotten what Dealmo told you in the tree house already? Do you have any idea how dangerous these people are? Even I wouldn't go in there on my own, and I can do back flips and climb like a spider monkey. Come on. You're going home. Your mum will be worried if she finds you gone.'

He turned and made for the exit.

'You don't know what it's like, being me.'

Fatyak stopped beside the door, frowning. 'What are you on about?'

'My dad's in prison, so people pick on me. I'm small, so I can't defend myself and I need other people to fight my battles for me. My mum keeps moving us around, so I never get to make friends.'

'We're friends.'

'No.' Rufus shook his head, his eyes

beginning to well up. 'You just feel sorry for me. If I had a superpower like you, I wouldn't need people to feel sorry for me. What if that cylinder they're after can give *me* a superpower like you guys?'

'Rufus, listen to me——'

'No, I'm done listening to people!'

The boy turned and bolted towards the crates.

⚡

Inside the museum, Colonel Bleach's voice interrupted the bleed of laser light that had cut three quarters of a perfect circle in the glass display.

'Say that again, guv?'

'There are two dots on the screen near the rear entrance and they're both heading your way.'

'Two *what*?'

Alvarez crowded in as Slud peered down the hall.

'Two moving dots,' Bleach confirmed. 'I've picked up nothing on the vehicle approach corridor in the grounds. Did you leave the storeroom open when you came in?'

'Yes, guv. I reckoned on a quick exit with all the security stuff. I turned those laser beams back on, though.'

'*Obviously*. That's why I received

the alert. I suppose it could be a glitch protocol for museum security, but I wouldn't take any unnecessary chances.'

Alvarez snatched the communicator from his colleague. 'I thought the guy you bribed was going to switch off all internal alerts so the police weren't called?'

'As I have already explained to you – twice – when I last spoke to our man on the inside, he had everything under control. Listen, it might be a couple of opportunists, and that would work greatly in our favour, especially if the police are triggered. Once you've grabbed the cylinder, you could knock the idiots unconscious and trap them inside the building to get the blame.'

Alvarez rolled his eyes.

'What sort of opportunists would wander into a high-security public building with a night guard? How do you know it's not the damn police?'

'Because I'm out front, because there aren't any officer patrols currently in the area and because our software tells us that no outbound call has been made to the authorities.' Bleach lowered his voice to a growl. 'Just bring me the cylinder, and make sure you don't leave a trail leading back to us. Nathan Heed messed up the last operation. I will not have incompetence striking twice on my watch. Stop thinking, Alvarez. JUST DO IT.'

Slud stared at the ceiling balefully as his colleague switched off the communicator and blew out a long, deep breath.

'How long have you and Clax worked for the Reach?' he asked as Slud carefully removed the glass and placed it at the foot of the display.

'Long enough. You got a problem with the Colonel's orders?'

'A problem with taking out some unknown interloper while we're supposed to be *robbing the place*? Yes, I have a problem. What if it's a couple of local street kids or something? I didn't sign up for this.'

'Maybe not ... but you *did* sign up.' Slud reached inside the case and lifted out the cylinder. Judging by the look on his face, it wasn't exactly lightweight. 'Just think of it in simple terms. Whoever just stuck their nose into our business is now standing between us and five hundred grand. Mind moving? We need to get out of this place.'

Alvarez held up a hand and fixed the communicator on to his belt. 'You stay here, guard the cylinder and collect up all the gear. I'll go ahead, find out what's happening and clear the way.'

⚡

'Rufus! STOP!'

Fatyak quickened his pace, putting on a burst of speed and silently conjuring every ounce of special energy he could muster. Then he diverted right, took a run up the wall and sprang off the brickwork with a kick that cast him on to the opposite wall. From there, he propelled himself down the corridor with a twisted somersault that carried him over Rufus's head and deposited him on the ground in front of the smaller boy.

Rufus cannoned off Fatyak's bulky frame and landed with an awkward groan.

'Listen,' said Fatyak, glancing over one shoulder as the first sliver of torchlight became visible at the end of the corridor behind him. 'I know we probably seem to have it all together, but you have to think about what you're doing. You're not just putting *yourself* in danger here.'

'I pressed the panic button! The others will be on their way.'

Fatyak sighed, shook his head and reached down to drag the boy to his feet. 'We have to get out while we still have a chance,' he said. 'Once we're clear of this place, we can talk about your problems.'

Rufus swiped Fatyak's arm away from him and glanced towards the end of the corridor at the emerging torchlight. 'I'm not scared! Do you hear me? I'm not scared of anything!'

He shrugged off Fatyak's renewed attempt to grab him and, in doing so, tumbled backwards and crashed into a large black vase half hidden in the shadows of the corridor.

The torchlight focused on the boy as he struggled to get up, while Fatyak let out an exasperated sigh and made a final, desperate grab for his friend.

'Run, Rufus! RUN!'

Reluctantly, Rufus seemed to come to his senses. He clung on to Fatyak and the pair made for the far door, but now the torchlight was coming from that direction.

'The other way! Go!'

They turned a second time and headed for the end of the corridor.

'This doubles back,' Rufus whispered. 'We have to—'

'DON'T. MOVE.'

7

The Hunt

Alvarez stepped out in front of them. Levelling his torch at the pair, he produced a small black box from his belt and pointed it at Fatyak.

'You two kids are in the wrong place at the worst possible time,' he whispered. 'You know what this is?'

Rufus felt a sudden flood of panic, his legs rooted to the spot with fear. Instinctively, he snatched hold of his friend's arm, but Fatyak wasn't moving. The older boy was just staring at the armed man with no detectable expression.

'It's a dart gun,' Alvarez explained. 'It can't kill you, but it can send you to sleep for a long time and, trust me, the feeling when those needles hit you really isn't pleasant.'

'Y-you have no idea how good the security system is here,' Rufus blurted. 'Y-you won't get more than three streets away before the police—'

'Shhhhh!' Alvarez put a finger to his lips. 'Don't speak, don't talk, don't even move. Just listen.'

Fatyak felt his heart pounding in

his chest, but he could only think of Rufus and the fact that the young boy had only found his way into this situation because the Outcasts had taken an interest in him. A cold shiver racked his body, and he found his throat dry when he tried to swallow. Still, he was trying hard to show no outward signs of distress.

'My employer wants me to lock you two away and stitch you both up for robbing this place, but I've got a conscience and I'm not going to do that. I'm telling you this because the man I'm working with will not hesitate to comply with our employer's instructions, not for a second. Do you understand, big guy?'

Rufus made to interrupt, but Fatyak snatched hold of his arm and nodded. 'Yes. I — we understand.'

'Good. Now, I want you to go into the room over there with the blue door and lock yourselves in. It's the security office and you'll be able to see us on the cameras, so you'll know when we're gone. After that happens, you and your little mate can leave and get on with your lives. I don't have time to repeat any of that, so I really hope you were listening. Now, GO.'

Fatyak took several steps backwards, dragging Rufus with him. They disappeared through the door and closed it behind them.

Alvarez didn't lower his weapon until he'd heard the lock click.

Then he turned on his heel ... and walked right into Slud.

'Whoa! How long have you been skulking in the shadows?'

The big man sighed and gritted his teeth.

'Long enough to recognise one of those kids, Alvarez. Now, give me the dart gun.'

'What are you talking about?'

'GIVE ME THE DART GUN OR I'LL TAKE IT.'

They both tensed, the little man

looking around him wildly as if some sort of solution was hanging in the air, waiting to be grabbed.

It was then that Alvarez noticed the security camera directly above them.

He held up the weapon, flipped it round and then handed it, very slowly and deliberately, to Slud, who managed to heft the cylinder under one arm and snatch the weapon with the other.

'Listen, we can't just—'

'No, *you* listen. You're here to do a job, just like me. If you can't do it, then perhaps you shouldn't be on the team.'

'Y-you needed me to get in here!'

'Yeah ... but now we're in, and I'm

left to clean up your mess. Go and report back to Bleach. I'll deal with the kids.'

'B-but ...'

'GO.'

Alvarez turned on his heel to make for the exit, but Slud shot him with a dart. He staggered, fell against the wall, slid a little way along the corridor and then hit the ground like a sack of potatoes.

Slud raised the communicator to his mouth. 'Colonel, we've got a big problem.'

⚡

In the manager's office, Fatyak stared

closely at the bank of monitors that covered the front hall security cameras.

'Rufus,' he said quietly. 'Life isn't like comic books, you know.'

'I said I was sorry,' Rufus snapped, his hands still shaking. 'I guess I'm looking for something. I suppose I just wanted to feel a bit ... you know ... special.'

'Yeah, well ... you might end up getting your wish in the worst way.'

Rufus tried to force a weak smile.

'Hey,' he said. 'At least the guy seemed like he didn't want to hurt us. I reckon—'

'They just had an argument,' Fatyak muttered, staring at the cameras.

'The man who pointed the dart gun at us just had a dust-up with another guy I'm pretty sure I recognise, and he's on the floor outside. The other guy's gone off camera. We need to barricade ourselves in.'

Fatyak grabbed a chair and wedged it under the handle of the office door. 'Help me, will you?'

Rufus thought for a moment. 'No! Don't bother!' He grabbed his friend by the arm and propelled him towards another door at the end of the room.

'What are you doing?' Fatyak protested. 'We have to block the door!'

'No! We need to get in the

restoration vault! It's the most secure room in the museum, and it locks from the inside! C'mon!'

They dashed out of the room and took a sharp right, just as a new flash of torchlight beamed out and two darts whizzed by them.

The pair threw a left turn and pelted down the new corridor with Rufus leading the way. The next passage was full of doors and double doors as far as the eye could see. Fatyak groaned inwardly, but Rufus showed no signs of hesitation. The boy found the main stockroom on his second attempt, dragged his friend inside and slammed the door behind them.

Rufus locked the latch that secured the room and headed to the far wall, where he pulled down a heavy metal lever and stepped back seconds before an entire section of the wall slid aside.

'This is it!' he said, his voice tinged with relief. 'Quick!'

They moved beyond the barrier, dragging the door shut behind them. When the massive lock rotated into position, Rufus stared in confusion at the computer pad on the wall. Fatyak watched him.

'I thought you knew loads about this place ...'

'Yeah, I do ... but my mum never

told me about security panels on vault doors!'

'If in doubt, leave it alone,' Fatyak warned. 'We've pulled the lock. Let's just wait and hope the others arrive.' He moved to stand behind Rufus and squinted above the panel. 'Is that a fire alarm?'

'Yeah,' Rufus said. 'I think so.'

'Good.'

Fatyak struck out with an elbow and smashed the glass.

$\lightning$

As a loud alarm began to sound throughout the halls of the museum, Slud exploded through the stockroom door and crossed to the vault. As he made his way through the room, he deposited the cylinder on the desktop.

'Are you sure?' came Colonel Bleach's rasping voice. 'Because unless you're one hundred percent on this, I want you and that cylinder *out* of the museum.'

'It's the one who destroyed the box, guv,' Slud muttered. 'I'm telling you, you can't mistake this kid. He's almost the same size as me.'

'Is there any sign of the others?'

Slud raised the communicator

again. 'No. The kid he's with seems ordinary enough ... but you know this bunch. How far away can the others be?'

He hammered a fist on the vault door and frowned.

'How long until you can shut this alarm off?'

As he spoke the words, the ringing cacophony abruptly ceased, its echoes slowly dying away in his ears.

⚡

'We have time. I've sent false alarm signals and two different cancel codes to all three emergency services.'

'The kids are in the restoration vault and they've locked the door. Is there an override?'

'Wait,' Colonel Bleach muttered in the background before his voice crackled on. 'Clax knows about the vault. He's going to read you a series of lock interrupts. One of them should work. Bring the kid who destroyed the box to me. Leave the friend inside. Where is Alvarez?'

'He was a problem, sir.'

'Fine. Just hurry up and get back here with the cylinder.'

⚡

Rufus felt his heart beginning to beat fast in his chest. Fatyak's worried expression filled him with a terror that wasn't dissimilar to the fear he'd felt when Todd Miller first whispered to him during the history lesson that now seemed like such a distant memory.

'W-why do you think the alarm stopped?'

Fatyak swallowed, placed his ear to the door and tried to listen. 'I don't know, but I'm guessing the guy outside had something to do with it. C'mon — forced entry, laser beams and alarms that shut down after three seconds? I reckon the Reach have cut this place off, isolated it.'

'B-but the police will already know, right?'

Fatyak shrugged, rubbed his eyes and looked down.

'Jeez. I'm still in my pyjamas.'

Rufus laughed nervously. 'If the Reach can isolate the museum, do you think they might also be able to get in here?'

Fatyak turned and peered around him. 'Rufus,' he said. 'I need you to hide.'

'What? *Where*? HERE?'

'Anywhere. The room looks like it opens up at the back. Find a box or a crate or something. I'm going to get behind the painting at the end.'

8

Midnight Rampage

Jake flipped open his mobile phone, checking his watch in the process.

'It's nearly one o'clock in the morning,' he said, when Kellogg's weary voice echoed over the line. 'Do you think it's been pressed by accident?'

'No chance. It's not the single tone we got from Fatyak's old one when he rolled on top of it. This was going constantly, like he was pressing it all the way to the museum. Then it just stopped.

I'm telling you, the kid's in trouble. I've spoken to Lemon and she's on her way.'

'What about Fatyak?'

'His phone was off, and the idiot wouldn't take another alarm, would he? I left a message.'

Slud tapped furiously at the control panel.

'NO! Again!'

'... 7432 3342 2817.'

'No.'

'Are you sure you typed it in right?'

'Clax, I swear to the Gods if you

say that one more time I will—'

'OK, OK. Try 2142 3532 5421.'

There was a moment of hesitation.

'No good. Look, this is mental. How many more are there?'

'Just two. Try 3522 34 22 6431.'

'You already gave me that one.'

'Oh, right. How about 3452 4521 1331?'

Slud punched in the code and stood back as the vault door hissed open. Then he quietly checked that the cylinder was squarely positioned on the desk, put two more darts in the gun and made his way into the room beyond.

The vault was basically a storeroom

with a few tables in the middle and stacks of free-standing shelving units along both walls.

There weren't many places to hide, and Slud almost found himself feeling sorry for the kids when he heard the distinct sound of breath being measured in the silence.

He grimaced, crossed the room in several vast strides and pulled the painting on to the floor.

There was nothing behind it.

A sound from the opposite end of the room caused Slud to spin round, his eyes searching the shelves for any signs of movement. A strange sort of beeping noise — the type made by an old-fashioned digital watch — was resounding repeatedly from somewhere near the door.

Slud made for the sound but, halfway along the unit on the right-hand wall, a vase tipped off the shelf and smashed on the floor, halting his progress.

He pointed the dart gun and released two needles into the back of the unit but, disappointingly, this resulted in no sudden screams.

Slud dropped on to his hands and knees before lowering himself on to his belly. Peering underneath the units on both sides, he saw no feet ... only boxes.

Sighing despondently, he picked himself up, muttered a few savage swearwords and, taking hold of the edge of its metal frame, sent one of the giant shelving units crashing to the floor.

Crates, urns, vases and statues cascaded from the shelves as they fell, smashing and splintering, on to the floor.

Slud whistled between his teeth and wondered briefly at the cost of the damage he'd just caused before moving on to the next unit.

If anything, this one hit the ground even harder, accompanied by a thundering crash that drowned out the irritating buzzer, but only for a second.

There was still no sign of the boys.

Slud flew into a rage, dragging down units on both sides of the room until there were only two left, one on either side of the vault door.

Infuriatingly, the beep was still going, but it sounded a lot louder as Slud padded up to the first of the two units and clamped a hand on the metal support. He could now hear another sound beneath the beeping, an undertone of fear once again: the rise and fall of laboured breathing.

Slud smirked and pulled on the unit with all his might, but it wasn't just crates that hit the ground.

Fatyak back-flipped over Slud's head, rolled sideways and delivered a kick to the crease in the back of the big man's leg, folding him up like a deckchair.

Slud cried out as he tried to turn on the base of his other leg, and raised the dart gun.

Fatyak kicked it out of his hand.

'Rufus!' the boy shouted desperately, as Slud snatched hold of his leg. 'Run! I mean it! *Ruuuun!*'

The smaller boy peered out from the edge of the last unit and made a break for the door.

Slud regained his footing and drove Fatyak into the wall. He snatched up his gun, firing the last few darts as quickly as possible, but Rufus was out of the vault and back inside the security office.

'Damn it!' Slud boomed, putting all his weight on Fatyak and forcing the boy into a rough headlock. 'Get back in here, you little creep, or I'll finish your friend *real* slow.'

'DON'T LISHEN!' Fatyak yelped, wriggling to get free. 'JUSHT GET OUT!'

Slud smiled as he heard the young boy hesitate in the room beyond.

'That's right, kid!' he shouted again. 'You don't want your bezzie mate, here, to suffer.'

As Rufus appeared at the vault doorway, Fatyak almost choked in an effort to escape Slud's grip. The boy was carrying the cylinder in his arms.

'I know who you are,' he said boldly, clutching the artefact as if it was the most important thing in the world. 'You work for the Reach. My friends told me all about you.'

Slud frowned, but his gaze quickly returned to the cylinder.

'Put it down and come over here,' he growled, tightening his iron grip on Fatyak's neck, 'or you're going to see something you'll remember for the rest of your—'

'This is heavy,' Rufus interrupted. 'But it's not *that* heavy. I can still run with it. You hurt my friend, you'll never get your hands on this thing.'

'You wouldn't *dare*.'

Rufus didn't even stop to think. He bolted from the room just as Colonel Bleach's voice came crackling over the communicator.

'Slud! What the hell are you doing in there? Where is my CYLINDER?'

Slud cursed under his breath, but the noisy distraction was enough to weaken his grip on Fatyak, who stamped on the big man's foot and twisted out of the headlock.

Enraged, Slud bellowed loudly and made a grab for Fatyak's shoulder. His grasping fingers found only air, however, as Fatyak had climbed the wall and was hanging from the fluorescent light fitting overhead.

'The skills from Pandora's box haven't completely deserted you then,' he snarled, staggering slightly as he righted himself. 'Think how powerful you'd be right now if you hadn't destroyed it.'

Fatyak swung himself into a somersault and landed beside the only bookcase still standing in the middle of the room.

'The rest of the gang will be here

soon,' he said, sounding more confident than he felt. 'You should slither out of this place while you can.'

Slud charged the stack, shouldering down a line of thick crates that toppled the bookcase and sent Fatyak tumbling on to the wreckage. He tried to twist aside but couldn't adjust his movement in time, ending up in a crumpled heap on the floor.

'One down,' Slud muttered. Then he hurtled out of the vault after the other boy.

⚡

Colonel Bleach held on to the back of the passenger seat as Clax began to move the van. They drove straight up on to the pavement outside the museum.

'Keep the engine running,' Bleach barked. 'I can see that if I want something doing properly, I'll have to do it myself.'

He drew a narrow pistol from a slot on the back of the seat and marched towards the museum.

Clax watched him go and then switched the van radio to the local police frequency. After a few minutes, he concluded that no dispatch patrol was being sent to the museum and thus he began, very slowly, to relax.

He turned on his mobile and reached for the packet of crisps he'd stashed in the glove compartment. Unfortunately, he'd only just put the first one into his mouth when he glanced through the windscreen and practically spat it out again.

Three of the Outcasts were running up the road towards the museum.

134

9

Bolt From The Blue

Claxon locked eyes with the girl — *that* girl — and his mind flashed back to the fight he'd had with her in her garden where everything had started to go so badly wrong for the Reach.

Claxon suddenly felt every punch she'd rained on him, every piece of glass that cut his flesh as she'd propelled him headfirst through that enormous ground-floor window.

His mind raced, but his body

reacted to the mountain of cowardice that dwarfed his inner courage. He slammed his foot on the accelerator and drove the van directly at the group.

'We're nearly there,' Kellogg said, holding the tiny digital screen up to the light. 'He must be inside the museum.'

'At midnight? I told you this was—'

'Kellogg! Dealmo! TRUCK!'

Jake and Kellogg both dived aside, but Lemon leaped on to the front of the van, a grim expression on her face. She snatched hold of the windscreen wipers as the truck swerved on to the road. When she saw Claxon's demented face behind the windscreen, a terrible recognition flashed in her eyes.

'It's them!' she screamed, reaching back with a balled fist to smash the glass. 'The Reach! Get inside!'

Claxon slammed on the brakes, and Lemon flew back on to the road. She landed awkwardly, rolling over backwards and ending her journey on the edge of the pavement. As she struggled to her feet, Claxon roared forward again, but she dived aside and the van jumped the pavement, narrowly avoiding the wall of the museum as it swerved around in a wild arc.

Lemon was on the truck like a spider, snatching hold of the side door-handle and wrenching on the lock until it snapped and the door slid open.

Claxon shifted the truck into reverse, but as he tried to back it up Lemon snatched hold of his collar and dragged him into the shadowy depths of the vehicle.

Scrambling to hold on to every fixture and fitting on the way, Claxon frantically wriggled free from the girl's iron grip, ripping his coat in the process. He threw two closed fists at Lemon, but she blocked them both and snapped her head forward with such force that the blow knocked Claxon through the open door of the truck. He hit the road in a crumpled heap and lay still.

⚡

Bleach skidded around the corner of the museum's central corridor and raised a sleek-looking weapon, only to find himself face to face with Slud, who appeared at the far end of the same passage, mirroring the action with his own torch and dart gun.

'Where is it?' Bleach snapped. 'Where is the cylinder?'

Slud sighed. 'The kid's got it.'

'I gave you *one* job to do.'

'Alvarez messed this operation up

for all of us,' Slud moaned. 'You'd have the cylinder by now if he hadn't gone soft over those kids.'

Bleach rolled his eyes. 'Just *find* the boy. I want my cylinder.'

⚡

Rufus huddled behind a corner display in the Greek section of the museum, palms sweating and hands shaking – trying desperately to avoid making the slightest noise. He released each breath in a thin, tight-lipped sigh, but the blood pumping in his temples made his skull reverberate with a noise that in his panicked state he felt sure was projecting as a deafening roar.

Please be OK, Fatyak, please be OK.

Rufus tried to banish the horrible visions from his mind, and focused on the cylinder instead.

It looked like the kind of tube that might be used to house a magnum of champagne, except that it was obviously made of pure gold. In this respect, the weight of the cylinder was off: it was heavy, but not as heavy as it should have been. It was as if there was something inside, helping to offset the burden.

Rufus studied the surface to see if he

could make out any marks or inscriptions, but there were none. As he turned the thing over, two sets of footsteps echoed in the hall, and he suddenly heard voices.

'Are you sure?'

'Yes, he's here. Look at the dot on the screen!'

'Rufus? You in here?'

Dealmo, Kellogg.

Rufus crawled from behind the display.

'Thank God,' he said. 'I thought you'd never come!'

Kellogg ran up to the boy and knelt beside him, while Jake maintained a careful watch on the corridor that fed a path to the display section.

'Are you OK?'

'Y-yes, I am. It's Fatyak! He's—'

'Fatyak's here?'

Rufus nodded. 'The big guy from the Reach got hold of him. They're after *this*!'

He tried to lift the cylinder into Kellogg's arms, but the gangly youth shook his head and backed off.

'Dealmo will protect you. We'll go and find Fatyak. Where is he?'

Rufus pointed with his chin.

'Restoration vault. It-it's on the first right, second left. You can't miss it, but you'll probably run into the big guy.'

'Don't worry about that,' Kellogg called in a hushed voice. 'We'll deal with *him.*'

Jake put a hand over the cylinder and concentrated.

'Open,' he said.

A blue light began to emanate from his palm. It spread outwards over the cylinder and quickly engulfed the entire length of it. There was a fizzle and a brief flash, then the room darkened once again.

Jake frowned. 'Hmm ... it won't open. There's definitely something in there – I can feel the energy it's giving off – but whatever it is, it's far too powerful for me to draw it out. Let's take this thing with us. We can worry about it afterwards.'

'Too late, Dealmo! Too late! Look!'

Colonel Bleach and Slud stood outlined in the archway that marked the entrance to the display. Slud had a self-satisfied smile on his face, but Bleach wore a pained, furious glare.

'Jake Cherish,' he said, spitting the words as if they were an accusation. 'At last we meet. I am Colonel Bleach, field commander of the Reach.' He produced the narrow taser and slowly raised it in front of him. 'Hand over the cylinder, CHILD. You have interfered with our affairs for the last time.'

145

Jake sighed and rose wearily to his feet. 'We'll see about that, old man,' he said. 'Rufus! GET DOWN!'

There was a sudden flash of light.

'Shoot him!' Bleach snapped, aiming his weapon. 'Shoot the boy now!'

Slud drew his dart gun and frowned.

'Which one's the right one?' he shouted.

Bleach blinked twice and rubbed his eyes.

Jake Cherish had multiplied tenfold ... and each identical boy was clutching an identical cylinder.

⚡

Fatyak was just regaining consciousness when he felt a strange warmth in his shoulder that seemed to spread out, flooding his entire body.

He opened one bleary eye and peered up into the face of a gangly boy with prominent front teeth and a jaw built for grinning. It took him a few seconds to recognise his friend.

'Don't worry, Yacker,' Kellogg said softly. 'You just landed a bit hard.'

'Don't I always?'

'Exactly.'

Fatyak suddenly twisted onto his hands and knees and began to clamber to his feet.

'Is everyone here?'

'Yeah,' Kellogg whispered. 'The whole gang.'

⚡

Slud and Colonel Bleach were firing darts and taser-wires in every direction. While the big henchman's pistol was quickly emptied, his panicked employer had taken careful aim in entirely the wrong direction. One extremely loud shot went wild, the wired pin hitting a glass barrier that shattered and irreversibly triggered the museum's main alarm: every lighting system in the building suddenly powered into flickering life.

Each time the Reach agents hit one of the Jake clones, the projected image simply flickered and moved around them. Wherever the real boy was, they certainly weren't having much luck finding him.

'I'm out,' Slud shouted suddenly, his pistol clicking. He reeled back and hurled the empty weapon at a random Jake, swearing under his breath when it passed right through the boy.

Colonel Bleach produced a second weapon and fired two more wires, then ran directly at the version of Jake he suspected had been standing right in front of him when the illusion was cast.

At the last second, however, he had a sudden moment of doubt and paused, offering the boy just enough of a hesitation for Bleach to discover he'd been right all along. Jake swung the cylinder upwards and caught the Reach officer under the chin with it.

Bleach staggered back with the sheer force of the blow, folded on to his knees and collapsed, his eyes rolling back in his head. At first, he lay still. Then he twitched a few times, before slithering on to his stomach and beginning to crawl away.

Slud charged at Jake, but only got halfway across the floor when Lemon appeared and struck him so hard that he flipped 180 degrees and hit the floor like a slab of meat.

She brought a foot down on his back while he was still gasping for air.

'We need to get out of here,' she shouted as the cloned images flickered and faded and Dealmo reappeared next to a frightened, bewildered Rufus. 'I can hear sirens!'

'He's the leader of the Reach!' Jake practically barked the statement, thrusting an accusatory finger at the retreating form of Colonel Bleach before raising the cylinder dramatically in front of him. 'They were after *this* thing.'

Lemon looked down at the cylinder and shook her head. 'We can't take it,' she said darkly. 'It belongs to the museum. Besides, we need answers. Not more questions.'

Kellogg appeared, out of breath, at the edge of the exhibit. He was followed by Fatyak, who was still staggering slightly and massaging his wrists with the pads of his fingers.

'Wh-what's happening?' Kellogg demanded, eyeing the cylinder in Jake's hands. 'It sounds like the police are outside.'

'Don't you understand?' Jake snapped at Lemon. 'This is our leverage.

We can't let it go!'

'We can't let *him* go,' she shouted back, pointing at a heavy iron door that Colonel Bleach had thrown open in order to make his escape.

Kellogg hurried over to it and peered into the shadows beyond.

'It goes down into the basement!' he said. 'C'mon!'

Fatyak joined him and the two of them hurtled down the stairs after Bleach.

⚡

Lemon and Rufus were staring at Jake, who was staring down at the cylinder with a wild, questioning expression.

'Dealmo,' she said quietly. 'Listen, the police will get the Reach for everything that's happened here. Rufus will stay put to back up our story and I don't doubt his mum will be able to help. Right?'

Rufus nodded vigorously. 'Mum will totally believe me. She always knows when I'm telling the truth.'

'If that all goes to plan,' Lemon continued, 'then our only option here is to get our answers from Bleach before the police arrest him. And, Dealmo, they're already here.'

She waited for Jake to react, but the boy had closed his eyes and his forehead was creased in grim concentration. A single, sharp yellow light was visible around his fingers. It slid over the cylinder like a thick stream of treacle, surrounding the boundaries of the object and glowing with a sickly tinge that flushed from yellow to green and back again.

Lemon swore under her breath and turned towards Rufus.

'Make sure *he* gets out before the police arrive,' she said, bolting after Kellogg and Fatyak.

Rufus couldn't take his eyes off

Jake, who suddenly seemed to have taken the form of an ancient sorcerer in a classic fantasy film: smoke poured from his nostrils and trailed away.

Then it happened. Jake's fingers sank into the golden lid, which slowly swallowed his entire arm.

Rufus stood fast, his jaw dropping and his eyes wide.

'What is it, Dealmo? Does it hurt? Are you OK?'

'Hold on,' Jake whispered, his face contorted with concentration. 'It-it's moving.'

He closed his eyes, twitched a few times and then slowly withdrew his hand. The resulting sight was so stark and surreal that Rufus almost lost the ability to speak. For against all realms of possibility, Jake Cherish was clutching ...

'A lightning bolt!' Rufus shouted. 'An actual lightning bolt. It's so bright, it's like looking at the sun!'

Jake narrowly opened his eyes, half looking away from the object.

'By all the gods,' Rufus gasped, stepping back and pointing at the boy. 'I-I think you're holding the weapon Zeus used to enslave the Titans.'

Jake said nothing, but proffered the glowing handful forward, twisting it slightly in his fist. 'I-I can barely hold it. T-take the cylinder. Now!'

Rufus lunged forward to cradle the heavy object, and practically went down with it as the weight brought the thing clanging to the ground. Fortunately, it remained intact.

Jake shook himself from his reverie and placed his free hand on the smaller boy's shoulder.

'You're an incredible kid, Rufus ... and one day very soon we're going to need you to be the Outcast that comes and saves us all. But not today. Today, you have to stay here and cover our backs.'

He smiled, nodded a swift goodbye and dashed off through the basement door, energy discharging all around him from the thunderbolt.

10
The Drop

Fatyak and Kellogg ran along a metal walkway that snaked over the vast expanse of the museum basement. Fatyak stopped first, climbing the barrier to get a better view of the floor plan.

'This place is like that room at the end of the first Indiana Jones movie!' Kellogg gawped. 'We'll never find him in here!'

Fatyak leaped the barrier and plunged an impossible distance before landing on his feet, on top of an enormous metal container.

'I'll take the long way then!' Kellogg shouted, locating a zigzag staircase that ran from the walkway to the basement floor. 'You stay up that end! I'll go towards that obelisk thing by the freight lift!'

Kellogg ran round the boundary of the basement, peering down each aisle as he passed. There was no movement that he could detect, but any sounds were quickly drowned out by the deafening clatter of Fatyak leaping from platform to platform as he crossed the basement via the haphazard, sprawling network of containers.

'Anything?' Fatyak boomed, appearing on the top of the box directly behind Kellogg.

'No! Wherever he is, he's well hidden!'

A sudden eruption of sound above and behind them signalled the arrival of Lemon, who emerged from the museum door and hurried along the upper walkway. 'He's not going to hide unless he has no other options!' she shouted. 'The police are here. Trust me, he'll try to get out!'

Kellogg put on a burst of speed and crossed from one end of the basement to the other, crouching down to look under every table and craning over each exhibit to see if any might afford Bleach a place of concealment.

'Come out, you COWARD!' Fatyak shouted.

'Where does that door go?' called Lemon, reaching the bottom of the staircase and heading for the freight elevator. 'It's open!'

Fatyak got there first, pushing the door wide and squinting at the fluorescent blur beyond.

'It's some kind of motor room for the lift,' he said, 'but it's small ... really small. If he's in there, it's not going to be difficult to find him.'

The vast majority of the room was occupied by a hydraulic engine that the group quickly circumnavigated as they spread out, Fatyak and Kellogg crawling on all fours in the narrow space, while Lemon kept watch at the front of the room.

'There's a glow,' Fatyak muttered.

'I see it too,' Kellogg confirmed. 'Has Bleach got some sort of cosmic weapon on him?'

'The glow isn't coming from Bleach,' Lemon shouted, her voice beginning to shake a little. 'It's ... coming ... from ... Dealmo.'

'What?'

'Where *is* Dealmo?'

Fatyak and Kellogg almost met nose to nose at the back end of the engine, and both leaped to their feet.

Lemon was staring at the door, where Jake had appeared.

He was bathed in white light and carrying ...

'Is that an actual bloody thunderbolt?' Kellogg shouted, his expression a mask of fascinated horror.

'Yeah,' said Jake, a sickly grimace on his face. 'It doesn't like me though. I'm starting to feel a bit puke-fest.'

'Great!' Lemon rolled her eyes. 'Another superpower we can't control.

Any sign of Bleach?'

'Yeah, we might have a problem there.' Fatyak pointed into the darkest corner of the room at a wide iron cage that yawned open, a padlock hanging from it. 'Looks like he found a way out after all.'

Beneath the cage was an open manhole cover.

⚡

Rufus emerged from the museum in the company of a single solitary policewoman and they walked against a steady tide of officers sweeping into the grounds.

Flashing lights and sirens turned the area into a scene from a movie set, and Rufus winced as he spotted another Reach agent hanging from the rear door of a damaged van by a single cuff, his head bowed towards the floor.

'Rufus? Rufus! THAT'S MY SON!'

Two officers parted to reveal the frantic face of Rufus's mother, who literally charged across the concourse and snatched him up in a hug so powerful that it actually hurt.

'Are you OK?' she asked, her eyes streaming with tears. 'Are you OK?'

'Yes, Mum! I'm fine!' Rufus tried to keep his voice steady as she drew away and looked him in the eyes. 'I'm so sorry, Mum. I'll tell you everything, I swear.'

⚡

An ocean of rats streamed away from the light as dank, wet corridors that hadn't been properly illuminated for years were suddenly awash with the powerful electric blaze of the thunderbolt.

At every junction, Fatyak and Kellogg peered left and right, on some occasions venturing a little way down the sprouting tunnels just to see if they could make out any signs of movement that didn't come from the nocturnal inhabitants of the sewer.

Lemon took the lead, walking some way ahead of the group and scouting out the longer passageways, in order to direct the group away from any danger zones. There were quite a few of these: tunnels that ended abruptly or dropped away, mini-waterfalls that spilled into deeper sections of the sewer.

'I thought the smell would be worse,' Kellogg said as Jake leaned over the side. 'It's actually not that bad down here if you consider that – Dealmo?'

Jake was dry heaving, clutching his stomach and making a tortured face, his cheeks puffed out and his eyes watering.

'Take it,' he implored, turning

to Kellogg and reaching out with the thunderbolt. 'It might be my power, but this thing is definitely hurting me. You might just be able to handle it with your ... you know ... ability.'

Kellogg looked horrified at the thought of touching the thunderbolt, but the pain and sickness on his friend's face spurred him on. He carefully closed a fist around the shining bolt and winced as a surge of energy ran through him. Bizarrely, it was like taking a warm bath: his entire body was submerged in the light. It felt fantastic.

'There!' Lemon spun round and beckoned the group. 'I see him! This way! QUICK!'

She hurtled down a corridor on the edge of the left-hand tunnel and disappeared from view. Jake and Fatyak gave chase.

Kellogg looked down at his hand, which had begun to shake quite violently. He felt no pain from the bolt, no heat and no damage, yet the main body of the artefact was definitely wriggling and morphing in his hand.

'Er ... guys?'

Suddenly afraid, Kellogg tightened his grip on the thunderbolt and tried to use his other hand to drag himself along the tunnel, but the strength of the bolt's thrusting effect drove him back. The tremor in his hand frantically increased and for a moment he thought the bolt might break free and take to the air.

Then something incredible happened.

⚡

'Bleach!'

Lemon, Jake and Fatyak skidded to a halt at the mouth of a junction. There, approximately halfway along the right-hand tunnel, was Colonel Bleach. Oddly, he was walking towards them.

'Stop right there!' Jake warned, a circle of blue light surrounding his open palm.

173

Lemon cracked her knuckles and Fatyak tensed as the vile man took one more step forward.

'I'm sorry it's come to this,' he muttered, his oily face shining in the reflected ripples of the sewer water. 'But there's a sheer drop at the end of that tunnel and I have to find another way out. You give me no choice but to go through you.'

'Good luck,' Fatyak spat. 'You'll give us some answers first.'

'What's happening to us?' Lemon shouted, her voice echoing through the tunnel. 'Why do we keep getting sick? Why do the powers keep coming and going?'

'How do we give it all back?' Jake asked in a measured tone. 'You know the answer. I can see it in your eyes.'

Colonel Bleach smiled, revealing crooked teeth beneath his twisted moustache. 'There were some words that might have helped, back before your friend smashed our property and sealed your fates.'

Fatyak flushed red, his lips curling up in anger. 'I had no choice. Nathan Heed would have killed us all if I hadn't destroyed it. You know he tried to take the power for *himself*, right?'

'Heed was a fool.' Bleach shrugged, snaked one hand into his jacket pocket and rummaged around inside. 'But what I tell you is true. Without the box, you can never give back your new lives: the good ... and the bad. I have it on strong authority that you're *cursed*.'

The pulsing blue light in Jake's hand took on a fiery edge. 'You're nothing more than a foot soldier,' he whispered. 'Who is really in charge of the Reach? Who do you all serve?'

Bleach removed his hand from the jacket and opened a palm to show the group a small, square box covered in arcane runes. 'You know what this is?' he asked, taking yet another tentative step forward and reaching up to block his ears with what looked like two small rubber plugs. 'I know it looks like an alarm but in fact it emits a signal that switches off certain types of energy. The bursts only seem to work for a few minutes at a time, but let me tell you something: I've taken down some very special individuals using this. You see, without all your magical powers you're just *children*.'

Bleach pressed the button, releasing what felt like a burst of electromagnetic energy. The entire tunnel flashed a blinding white, and a swirling, rhythmic noise grew in pitch until the group felt sure their eardrums were bursting. Then, just as suddenly, the noise and the light disappeared.

Colonel Bleach hit Fatyak with a rugby tackle that took the boy right off his feet and sent them both crashing into the wall of the sewer tunnel. Fatyak groaned and slid down on to his knees, while Jake recovered from the shock enough to charge Bleach with a flank attack.

The Reach commander caught Jake with an outstretched arm, twisted the boy's hand behind his back and, bringing a heel kick to bear on the crease of his knee, forced him to the ground.

Lemon screamed as she thundered down the tunnel mouth, striking out with a two-handed blow that would have driven

Bleach through the wall had her powers been intact. As it was, the Colonel caught her hands in a strong wristlock.

'I don't hit girls,' he muttered, 'but since I can't have you following me ...'

He twisted suddenly, using his body weight to flip Lemon over his head. She landed on her back in the narrow stream of water.

'You kids have got some courage,' Bleach spat, crossing the tunnel. 'I'll give you that.'

He snatched hold of Fatyak's collar. 'Do you know how hard I had to work to get that box? You ruined my credibility when you destroyed it, *boy*. Now you're going to pay ...'

A series of splashes made Bleach look up sharply, a quizzical frown on his face.

Kellogg appeared at the mouth of the tunnel, walking with a slow, unsteady pace and wearing a decidedly nervous expression.

'Oh yes,' Bleach oozed tirelessly. 'I'd forgotten there were four of you.' He shoved Fatyak aside as Kellogg advanced. 'It's so easy to overlook the one who gets the most useless ability, isn't it? I mean, from what I've been told, the box effectively turned you into a set of magic plasters, right? Hahahaha! I'd get out of the way if I were you.'

Bleach charged forward.

Just in time for Kellogg to raise a hand and hit the man with a lightning bolt.

The strength of the explosion as the searing dagger of energy left Fatyak's hand was enough to floor everyone in the tunnel and light up the sewer for half a mile. In the museum above, police officers found themselves looking to the windows and waiting for the sounds of thunder.

Colonel Bleach was lifted off his feet by the bolt and slammed into the end of the sewer wall. The electricity wracked his body and, failing to stand, he tried to crawl through the murky water on his belly, coughing and choking as he went. The charge of electricity all around him suddenly withdrew and sparked across the tunnel at incredible speed, only to be sucked back into Kellogg's outstretched hand.

The Outcasts collectively helped each other to stand, and stared at their friend with a new yet terrible respect ... but Kellogg seemed more angry about his new power than proud of it.

He walked straight past them and splashed along the tunnel after Bleach, who had crawled around a bend at the junction and disappeared from view.

'Kellogg,' Jake called as they started to stagger after him. 'Wait ...'

'Hey, man!' Fatyak tried. 'Hold on for us!'

Lemon pushed in front of them.

'KELLOGG!' she screamed. 'We can sort this out! Don't do anything stupid!'

Beyond the tunnel, the sewer expanded dramatically as myriad different channels intersected enroute to the waste-water treatment plant. Colonel Bleach had climbed awkwardly to his feet, turning to face the advancing figure of Kellogg, and was edging towards an enormous underground fall designed to sweep the main channel south.

'Y-you have no idea what you've done,' Bleach spluttered, his body still throbbing from the wave of electricity that had rushed through him. 'Th-the thunderbolt. Y-you absorbed it? B-but th- that's impossible!'

'It felt more like the thunderbolt absorbed *me*,' Kellogg said, reaching out a hand and pointing a single finger at Bleach. 'But my friends and I have suffered enough. You have one chance to tell me who gives you your orders.'

He shot out a small bolt of electricity, plunging Bleach's body into a spasm that almost sent him over the edge of the falls.

'P-please!' he screamed. 'I-I don't know his name! I don't know any of their names! I'm just a s-s-servant! I j-just take orders!'

Kellogg lowered his finger and stretched out an entire hand in its place.

'Where do you go to get them?' he said, this time sending out a bolt of pure white energy that made every muscle and sinew in Bleach's body erupt with pain.

The Outcasts emerged on the edge of the falls and quickly moved to surround their friend.

'STOP!' Fatyak shouted, raising his arms to throw Kellogg off balance and then thinking better of it. 'You'll kill him!'

'I'm waiting for an answer,' the boy said calmly, his voice clearer than crystal as the light blazed around him.

'Argghghgh!'

'An answer.'

'Arghghghghghh-ake Manor! DRAKE MANOR! Please – please stop!'

'Got it!' Fatyak practically yelled in Lemon's ear. 'He told us. Now stop!'

The boy took a breath, but he didn't lower his gaze and the stream continued to flow.

'Kellogg, you have to listen to me,' Jake snapped, almost stepping into the beam of energy. 'If you kill this idiot, we're no better than them. We're no better than *Nathan Heed*.'

'It's your fault, Jake.' Kellogg sent out flow after flow of lightning, every new bolt searing along the line of crackling energy. 'If you hadn't made us play that stupid game, none of this would ever ... have ... happened.'

'Kellogg, I'm here.' The words broke the boy's concentration and he immediately turned his horrified eyes to Lemon, who had walked up behind him with tears in her eyes and placed a single hand on his shoulder. As he turned, she wrapped her arms around his neck and enveloped him in a hug, but he just stared past her in wide-eyed disbelief at his own hands, as if they belonged to somebody else.

'I-I'm sorry, Lem,' he said. 'I'm sorry.'

'It's OK,' Lemon said softly. 'You managed to control it.' As she drew herself away, she was flooded with relief to see the familiar confused expression return to her best friend's face.

Released from the wash of energy, Colonel Bleach twitched, staggered slightly and, snatching at handfuls of air, managed to stay on his feet. He took one small, pathetic step sideways ... before Fatyak shoved him over the edge of the falls.

Jake, Lemon and Kellogg all rushed to the precipice, seconds before a distant splash echoed through the surrounding sewer.

They turned to look at Fatyak, who shrugged off all three accusatory stares.

'What?' he said. 'He landed in water, didn't he?'

189

Epilogue

The following Saturday morning, Rufus couldn't get to the games shop fast enough. He even took a shortcut through the storage yard and failed to feel even the smallest tingle of fear as he passed Todd Miller and the two goons who'd ambushed him just a week before.

When he finally pushed through the door and the little brass bell chimed overhead, he saw that the main gaming floor was full ... but there was no sign of the Outcasts. He checked his phone for the millionth time, but he hadn't received any texts.

Visibly deflated, Rufus made his way to the back of the room and, taking a deep breath, opened the old wooden door that led to the shop's small and solitary card pit.

Jake, Lemon, Fatyak and Kellogg looked up at him with a mixture of shock and delight.

'Oh hey, Rufus,' Fatyak muttered, looking up with tired eyes before starting to put out an extra hand of Munchkin. 'We wondered when you'd show up. I'll just deal you in for the next round.'

'Guys!' Slumping into the chair, Rufus could barely stop his heart beating with excitement. 'I'm so glad to see you all. You look ... er ... terrible.'

'We feel terrible,' Kellogg said, barely able to disguise his shaking hands. 'We're always weak after we use the power ... but it's worse, this time. We're not healing as fast.'

Lemon coughed suddenly, a horrible rasping whoop that didn't sound like it would ever stop. The girl practically doubled up in an effort to stop herself choking.

Jake hit Lemon sharply on the back to help her, before leaning across the table and staring Rufus right in the eye. For a time, he didn't speak.

'What? What is it, Dealmo?

I covered for you all, right? Nobody asked any questions?'

'You did us proud,' Jake confirmed, clasping a hand on Rufus's arm. 'But now we need you to do something much more important.'

As Fatyak stood to shut the door, the others huddled in close to the table.

'We need you to tell people about the things that happened to us, to *all of us*, if we don't come back.'

Rufus looked from Jake to Fatyak and from Lemon to Kellogg, but he didn't see the slightest glimmer of an explanation in their eyes.

'If you don't come back from

where?'

Jake drew in a deep breath. 'First, we need some time to get our strength back,' he said. 'And then we're going after the Reach. For real.'

ACKNOWLEDGEMENTS

Thanks to Sophie Hicks (agent), Anne McNeil (publisher) and Polly Lyall Grant (editor) for all their work helping to make this series a reality. Thanks also to my family reading team: Chiara, Barbara and Sebastian Stone. Lastly, thanks to Evie Stone for letting her daddy write when he should have been playing The Cupcake Game!

LOOK OUT
FOR MORE

OUTCASTS

ADVENTURES
COMING SOON ...

david grimstone

REVIEWS

"This book is different to the other books I have read and it kept me wanting to read more. I am reading it now for a second time."

POPPY HARRISON, AGE 9

"It's exciting and dramatic, but also sad. I can't wait to read the next book. It is going to be so cool!"

BEN WILLIAMS, AGE 9